# Sloop John B

For Matthew, Adam, Robbie, Drew and their

children's children.
–AJ

To Troy. Thank you for sailing the oceans with me.
–JP

A publication of
Milk and Cookies Press, a division of ibooks, inc.

ibooks, inc.
24 West 25th Street, 11th floor, New York, NY 10010

The ibooks, inc. World Wide Web Site address is:
http://www.ibooks.net

ISBN: 0-689-03596-9
First ibooks, inc. printing: May 2005

10 9 8 7 6 5 4 3 2 1

Editor–Dinah Dunn
Associate Editor–Janine Rosado

Designed by Edie Weinberg

Library of Congress Cataloging-in-Publication Data available

Manufactured in China

# Sloop John B

## A PIRATE'S TALE

## by Alan Jardine
## Illustrated by Jimmy Pickering

MILK & COOKIES PRESS™

New York

Distributed By Simon & Schuster, Inc.

**W**e come on the *Sloop John B,*
my grandfather and me.
Around Nassau town we did roam.

Sailing all night—
Woke up at first light—
It's time to get up,
see how far we've gone.

So hoist up the *John B's* sail!
See how the mainsail sets.
Wind in the sail, I feel her racing along.
Then we will roam—
On the ocean foam—
It's time to get up, see how far we've come.

**W**e sailed into a fog,
according to the captain's log.
That's when the pirate ship
came alongside.

I heard a voice roar,
"We're coming aboard."
I told my grandpa,
we both better hide!

The pirate,
he got the fits . . .
And threw away my grits!
Then he took and he ate up
all of my corn.

I almost cried.
I was hiding inside.
Then I saw a pirate,
asleep on the floor.

As I ran out the cabin door—
Picked up a pirate's sword—
That's when I saw my Grandpa
walking the plank!

Grabbed a line there,
and as I flew through the air
I pushed that pirate
right into the *drink!*

So hoist up the *John B's* sail—
See how the mainsail sets—
Call for the captain ashore,
let me go home.

Let me go home!
Why don't they let me go home?
Please tell those pirates to leave us alone!

The pirate he got dunked.
Then broke in the captain's trunk.
Constable had to come and
take the pirate away!

Now we can roam
on the ocean foam.
For me and my grandpa,
the ocean's our home.

We come on the *Sloop John B*,
my grandfather and me.
Around Nassau town we did roam.

Sailing all night—
Woke up at first light—
Me and my grandpa,
the ocean's our home.